Why Are You Calling Me a Barbarian?

Birgitta Petrén and Elisabetta Putini

Illustrated by Lara Artone and Monica Barsotti

Translated from the Italian by Mary Becker

The J. Paul Getty Museum • Los Angeles

At the J. Paul Getty Museum:
Christopher Hudson, *Publisher*
Mark Greenberg, *Managing Editor*
Shelly Kale, *Editor*
Kurt Hauser, *Designer*
Translation adaptation by Shelly Kale
With contributions from John Harris,
Benedicte Gilman, and Leslie Rollins

First published in the United States in 1999 by
The J. Paul Getty Museum, 1200 Getty Center Drive,
Suite 1000, Los Angeles, California 90049-1687

English edition © 1999 The J. Paul Getty Museum
© 1997 «L'ERMA» di BRETSCHNEIDER
Via Cassiodoro, 19–00193 Roma - Italia

Library of Congress Catalog Card Number: 99-13327
ISBN 0-89236-559-5

Printed in Italy

Contents

This book is dedicated to
our own little Europeans,
Johan, Anna, and Martina,
who are about to begin
their splendid adventures
in the world.

Martilla and Her Cow

My name's Martilla, and I'm nine years old. I live in Rome, but I've been traveling with my family for many months. How many? I've lost track. Since our last stop, I've walked seven hours. I'm exhausted, my tunic is dirty, and my sandals are torn.

I'm very, very cold. It's been getting colder and colder as we slowly head north. It feels like winter here, even when it's actually springtime. I miss the fragrant flowers of Rome, and my cozy home.

This is my cow, Rufola. I watch her, prod her along, milk her every evening, and look after her calf, too. It's a hard job! But thanks to Rufola, my master gave me permission to go along on this trip.

My master's a general in the Roman army. We're heading north, toward Cologne—I think it has something to do with a war.

My father's the general's favorite slave, and my uncle, Elio, is his cook. The general can't live without Uncle Elio's fine cooking, not even during a war.

I hear someone calling, "Martilla! Martilla! Your cow is slowing down!" Maybe I should climb on top of Rufola and let her carry me. Who knows how many more hours of marching are left before we reach Cologne?

Marbord the "Barbarian"

My name's Marbord, and I come from the part of the world the Romans call Scandia. It's very far north of Rome. I'm eleven years old, almost twelve. Even though I'm just a boy, these Romans think of me as their enemy. I'd better be careful! If they can, they'll capture me and carry me away as their slave.

My family are descendants of a Germanic tribe. The Romans call us "barbarians" because they think that we're stupid. Maybe they don't know that the word "barbarian" means "traveler" or "foreigner." To us the *Romans* are the foreigners. So that makes them barbarians, too, right?

I'm very proud of my name, Marbord. My father gave me this name so that I would become strong and wise like the famous leader Marbord who lived more than a hundred years ago. He was a chieftain who put together the biggest Germanic army ever to fight the Romans.

Marbord's army killed more than 15,000 Roman soldiers in the big, dark forest of Teutoburger. If you're not afraid of ghosts, you can still find rusty Roman swords and shields in that forest today.

My father's a merchant who buys and sells Roman arms. I watch out for thieves—they're everywhere—and help him keep everything in order. This job keeps me busy all day long.

Look at that strange little girl. She's riding a cow! So that's how these "noble" Romans travel!

Martilla Meets Marbord

Finally we're camped at Cologne. There's a strange boy here with funny clothes. His hair is funny, too: it's almost white, even though he seems just a little older than me! Now he's coming toward me and speaking my language, Latin.

The boy sure has a funny accent, and he makes a lot of mistakes, but he's using his hands to help him explain. He's pointing toward the river. At last I can have a cool drink, and so can Rufola and her calf.

That was refreshing! I asked the boy how he learned Latin. He told me that many, many years ago, a Roman leader conquered his land. Some of his soldiers married the women who lived there, mixing their customs and languages. I think the boy's talking about our emperor Marcus Aurelius. My grandfather told me a little about him.

The boy is eleven, and his name's Marbord. He seems nice enough, though a little strange. . . . I've decided to make friends with him because I'm actually a little lonely, and I'm also curious to find out more about his people. I have a lot to tell *him* about, too. I wonder if we'll be able to understand each other. . . .

Marbord Meets Martilla

The girl on the cow is named Martilla. Martilla! Back home I don't know anyone with that name. She's funny and nice and she laughs a lot. She reminds me a bit of my little sister, Freija.

I don't like it when Martilla teases me about not knowing the right word in Latin, or about my accent. Doesn't she realize it just means I speak one language more than she does? So maybe it's not so bad that we northerners have learned Latin, even though it's very hard. It would be great if everyone in the world spoke the same language; then maybe no one would be called a barbarian.

Martilla and I have an agreement: we're going to tell each other all about what life is like where we live. I'll tell her about Scandia, and she'll tell me about Rome. We'll even have a contest: whoever remembers the most about the stories we share with one another will be the winner.

Rome may be a grand place, but I'm going to show Martilla that there's no such thing as a barbarian.

A Special City

So you want to know how we Romans live? Well, first of all, life in the country is very different from city life. There's always a ton of work to do in the country, but life rolls along peacefully there.

City life is much more exciting, especially in Rome, which is the capital of our great empire. We all wake up at dawn and get right to work. The streets fill up with people, mules, handcarts, goods—the traffic and confusion are unbelievable! Every day new construction yards appear for the building of streets, houses, and monuments.

The Forum is the real heart of daily public life in Rome. It's a large square with splendid buildings and temples. Every day it's teeming with people—senators, lawyers,

even slaves—who go there to exchange goods, discuss business and politics, or just chat a little.

For lunch you can have a quick bite on the street or in the taverns. That way, business can go on until two or three in the afternoon. But many Romans spend their afternoons at the public baths, where they relax and meet friends. It seems like heaven to me! Just think, there are tubs with water at all temperatures, gymnasiums, saunas, and dressing rooms. What do you think about that?!

Finally, just before sunset, everyone goes home for dinner. That's because when night falls, the city's so dark and dangerous that it's safer to stay home.

Oh, my! It's gotten late, and Rufola's waiting to be milked!

Life in Our Village

Now let me tell you about *my* home! In the part of Germany where I live there 'aren't any big cities, only big or small villages. Each village has a chief, who is the richest man there. The chief makes all the decisions and is responsible for defending the village.

Our chief is strong and wise. He built walls around the village to protect us from our enemies on land, and he planted poles under the water to trap enemy ships.

We wake up at dawn, when the cock crows. We have to wake up early to work while there's plenty of daylight, because our houses are very dark. The only light we get is from the fireplace.

In our village, we do everything by ourselves. Everyone has to pitch in so that we'll have everything we need by the time winter comes.

around on his back for fun! I must have looked as funny as you do riding your cow!

Look, it's still light out. It would be nice to have one of your baths right now to wipe off all this dust and to get rid of the flies that are always hanging around Rufola. Why don't we jump in the river? Come on, last one in is a barbarian!

Usually we children spend the day weeding the fields or watching over the animals grazing nearby. It's really hard work, and you can't be lazy. That's why I'm happy when my father asks me to go with him on his trips!

Our village is pretty rich: we have cows, pigs, sheep, and goats. We even have horses! And we have dogs as big as rams who'll attack any unwelcome visitors. We feel very safe with them around. They're also expert hunters, and they always accompany the men during a hunt. When I was little, one of our dogs carried me

Houses of All Kinds

Achoo, achoo! What a terrible cold! You and your great idea—bathing in the river in this cold! We Romans are used to the heat. That's because the large city houses like the one I live in have a heating system.

I live in a big walled-in manor house called a *domus*, like all the rich and powerful people do. I live there only because all my relatives are slaves in the service of a wealthy general.

I'll draw you a picture of a domus so I can describe it better. See this? All the rooms look out onto a central outdoor courtyard called the *atrium,* which provides the light inside. The atrium is open on top. When it rains, the water is collected in a kind of basin dug into the floor and then used later on. In a separate corner there's a little altar that looks like a small temple, where my master prays to the spirits to protect the house.

Behind the domus is the place I like the most: a marvelous garden surrounded by columns. It's called the *peristyle.* It's a shady little corner where you can eat lunch and stay cool during the summer. It has vine-covered trellises and trees and bushes of fragrant herbs. The best rooms are near the garden. That's where my master sleeps.

But I almost forgot! There are also stables, a kitchen, a pantry, and a *latrina,* which has toilets and baths. There are

even oil lamps, which light up the house! The walls are painted with beautiful paintings called frescoes. And the floors are decorated with mosaics— little pieces of colored stone or glass that are pasted together to form splendid designs. I know a lot about mosaics because I often have to polish them. But why do you look so surprised?

Living out in the Open

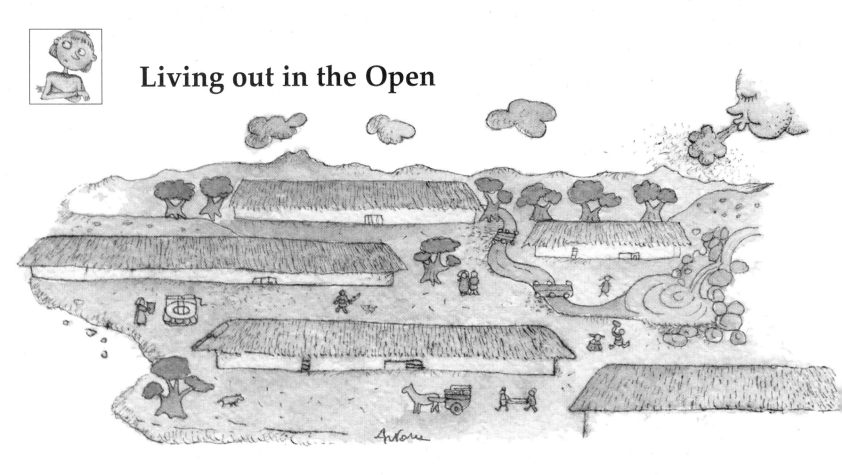

Do you have to ask? What you've told me sounds like a fairytale! Where I come from, the houses are low and very long, and the roof is like a hat that protects us from the cold and rain. In my land, there's almost always an easterly wind, so most of our houses are built to keep the wind behind us. They look like upside-down boats!

Our chief lives in the longest house in the village, almost 100 feet. My family's house isn't quite that long. I live there with my parents, my sister, my grandmother, my grandfather, and my great-grandfather. My great-grandfather's so old that he spends the whole day lying on a bench near the fire, which is always kept lit in the center of the room to keep the house warm. But still, he's always cold. He'd sure be happy if we had a heating system like yours!

We all sleep on benches along the walls, and we sit on the same benches when we eat. We have shelves way up high, just below the ceiling, where we keep our food so that the mice won't eat it.

Oh, I forgot to mention the animals! They also help to heat up the house. We keep them all inside—the pigs, the sheep, the goats, and the horse, too. They live in the right side of the house, and we live in the left side.

But those baths of yours sound strange to me. Do you Romans really take baths? At home I sometimes take a dip in the sea, but I only take a bath when my mother makes me. Fortunately, that doesn't happen very often!

Things to Make Your Mouth Water

Let's talk about something really special—like food! Roman food is really great. The city is full of markets and groceries that sell fruit, vegetables, spices, flour, meat, and fresh fish. Sometimes I go with the houseservant to do the shopping. We bring home delicious ingredients for Uncle Elio's recipes. Just thinking about them makes my mouth start to water!

In the bakeries you can buy fragrant round loaves made from flour, wheat, and barley, and baskets overflowing with crispy cookies and sweets. What I wouldn't give to have one now!

These are the meals we have each day: for breakfast we eat flattened focaccia bread spread with olives and cheese. For lunch, just bread with vegetables or mush made from flour.

The main meal is dinner. In rich families' homes, like ours, dinner begins around four o'clock in the afternoon. First the hosts and guests take off their shoes and wash their feet. Then they lean on cushions on the couches and feast on roasts, poultry, goat, pork, game, warm focaccia bread with cheese made from milk, eggs, mushrooms, sauces, cheeses with herbs, fish, vegetables, fruit, and as many sweets as they like! All the leftovers, bones, and skins are tossed onto the floor.

Then the meal is washed down with wine that has been mixed with water to make it weaker—we don't want our guests to get too drunk! Sometimes the wine is sweetened with honey.

We slaves run back and forth with the serving platters and the jars of wine. It's hard work! But sometimes we get to eat the leftovers when the banquet is over. Now I'm so hungry, I'm going to get something to eat!

How About Some Smoked Deer?

Wait just a minute! Do you really wash your feet before eating? Why on earth would you do that? Don't you eat with your hands like we do? Washing your feet—that's the strangest thing you've told me yet! We sometimes rinse off our fingers, but only after the meal is over.

Now I'll tell you what *we* eat. We have a lot of fresh fish. I catch some of it myself in the sea near our village. We have bread, and perhaps it's similar to yours, because we, too, grow barley, wheat, and rye. We also use a type of grain called oats to make mush or delicious cookies. There's nothing better than the smell of bread that has just come out of the oven!

Artoue

My mother mills the flour by herself, and Papa has just given her a brand-new mill. She uses two flat stones to crush the grain, turning them in opposite directions. She can mill a lot of flour that way.

We, too, eat the meat from sheep, pigs, cows, and wild game. I think that smoked deer is the best thing in the world! And we drink a whole lot of wine at our parties, but I think it's different from yours. One kind is made from fruit and another kind, called *mead*, is made from barley and hops and is sweetened with honey— just like yours.

But we don't dilute the wine with water. Maybe we should, because at our parties many grownups get so tired that they fall asleep before they can get up from the table. Then the slaves sneak up to the table to eat all the leftovers, just like yours do!

City Style

See how shabby I look! All my tunics are filthy here! Back in Rome, my clothes are neat and clean. My mama makes them. She's a first-rate weaver!

Most people in Rome don't weave anymore. They buy fabrics, such as silk, which is a very expensive and shiny cloth that comes from far away. Only the rich can afford it. But the lady of our house is a bit old-fashioned, and her maids spend hours at the loom making cloths of wool, linen, and cotton that can be dyed in any color you want. The most popular color is a purplish-red that comes from some kind of fish.

Around Rome you see all kinds of clothes because our fashions have been mixed together with those of the lands we have conquered.

Gentlemen wear a garment called a *tunic*, which is held closely to the hips by a beautiful belt. On top of the tunic they wear a *toga* in the shape of a half-moon. The toga is pinned to one shoulder with a *fibula* and then draped around the body, folded, rolled, and gathered up. It's quite a job!

Fashionable ladies wear the *stola*, a long, pleated dress gathered with two belts. They dress them up with embroidery and accessories and wear either a long or short cloak over their shoulders. And their makeup and hairstyles! I've seen ladies with hair that has been dyed and sprinkled with gold dust! Their heads look like bushes, with false curls tied up like a spool of thread or in the shape of a turtle. You wouldn't believe it!

Both men and women wear leather shoes, the *calceus*, with laces that climb up around the leg. At home, they wear sandals or comfortable slippers. But poor people and slaves wear only sandals made from untanned leather, with very hard wooden soles. And we don't wear togas, only tunics. It's a hard life!

We Trouser-wearing People

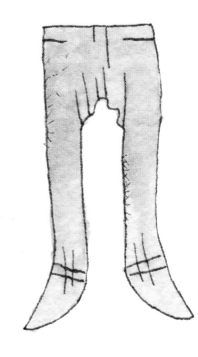

My father told me that you Romans call us "trouser-wearing people." You may think that our long pants make us look really funny, but they're actually a very clever invention.

In the winter, we wear these trousers down past our feet. That's how we protect ourselves from the freezing

cold. When it freezes over, we wrap bands of material over our pants and fasten them with belts of leather or wool. That way, we have two layers of cloth keeping us warm. But in the summer, we wear shorts and go around barefoot.

We also sew some loops on our pants to hold our belts in place. You can tell how rich a man is by how big his belt buckle is and the type of metal it's made of.

From the belt we hang some things that we use every day, like a knife or something to help us light a fire. I also wear a tunic and a fibula, like in your country. Our fibulae come in many different shapes. Some are even made in the shape of a serpent biting its own tail!

The women in our land wear long pleated skirts and a blouse, and a cloak when it's cold. Or else they wear strange dresses that look like tubing, and that are fastened over their shoulders with two fibulae. Poor things, they can't even ride horseback with those tubes on!

My mother weaves and sews everyone's clothes, just like the women do in your house. What a hard job! First the village sheep are shorn. For us children, that's the most exciting day of the year. It's our job to gather the sheep together and hold them while the adults clip their wool. Afterwards, they seem so naked and fragile!

Our sheep are brown, black, and white, and so our clothes are mostly these three colors. Have you seen my father? He wears a nice blue cloak, and yet there are no blue sheep. My mother dyes a part of the wool herself, and she makes it the color of the sea. Isn't that a beautiful shade? When I'm older, I hope to have such a cloak of my own.

Children Like Us

In every Roman family, the father makes all the decisions—even from the time a child is born. Some fathers decide not to keep their newborns and place them beneath a column for anyone to adopt.

Children are given a funny-looking pendant called a *bulla* to wear until they are older. I don't have a bulla, because I'm a slave.

But whether or not you're a slave, there's always time to play. And there are many types of toys to play with! Little children play with rattles made from terra-cotta or wood that are filled with little pebbles. For the bigger children there are hoops, balls, tops, and little wooden horses on wheels.

We children of slaves play outdoor games that are a lot of fun, such as hide-and-seek and blindman's bluff. And we build castles out of walnuts—I'll show you how!

This is my doll, Flora. She's made from wax and rags. Dolls that rich girls own have moveable arms and legs that seem almost real. They're not made from rags either, but from bones and terra-cotta, with hairstyles fit for an empress!

But I adore my Flora, and I wouldn't trade her even for a doll that's made of gold.

Roman children don't only play all day. They also go to school, even the girls. I don't go to school, but I learn lots of things from my grandfather, who's from Greece. Everyone says that the best teachers are from Greece. But they're also very strict. They hit students who don't behave or who are lazy with a rod called a *ferula*.

Many children learn in small groups of students at their teacher's home. But rich students, like my master's son, Lucio, have a private tutor. Lucio puts all his supplies in a *capsa*, a stiff bag shaped like a cylinder that holds rolls of paper for reading. He uses a pointed stick called a *stylus* to write on a tablet covered with wax.

But enough about school. Let's play a game of walnuts!

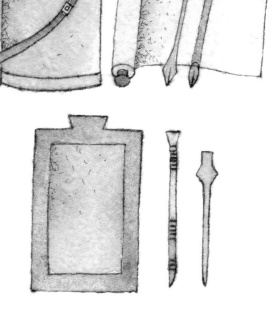

Life Without School

I had a lot of fun playing that game with the nuts! When I go back to my village, I'll teach it to my friends. And Flora is very cute. My little sister would love her. She seems so much more lifelike than the wooden dolls at home.

We don't have as many games as you do, but in some ways we're luckier—especially our newborns. We don't abandon them at the foot of a column! In our village, there aren't quite as many people as there are in Rome, so everybody needs everybody else, even us little ones. If there aren't enough children to grow up and become strong, and to look after their parents when they become old, what will happen to our village?

Oh, don't be sad! There's a lot more I can tell you about. Do you want to hear about school? We don't go to school! We learn everything we need to know at home.

My mother taught me how to treat sick people with herbs. I can treat stomach aches, and I even know how to stop a wound from bleeding. I bet Roman children don't learn that at school!

My father teaches me many important things, too: how to build a house, how to sow barley and wheat, how to chase a deer against the wind so it doesn't know you're there, even how to get the best price for our goods. All this is better than going to school, don't you think? And I don't have to be afraid of that terrible — what did you call it? *Ferula!*

Come on, let's chase each other! I'm faster than you. Catch me if you can!

Super Caesar

I want to tell you about a very famous Roman, Julius Caesar. Have you ever heard about him?

In life, he was a great and unique man. Even his death has become legend! He lived a very long time ago, the son of a noble family. During his lifetime he did everything under the sun. He conquered Gaul, fighting in the front lines. He narrated his adventures in a diary, *De Bello Gallico*, which later became a famous book.

He had three wives and many girlfriends. One of them—Cleopatra, the Queen of Egypt—was at least as famous as he was!

In Rome, Caesar was the greatest government official. Eventually, he became the leader of the Romans for life. In fact, his name, Caesar, is still used to mean "emperor."

Of course, he had many, many enemies, even in Rome. One of them stabbed him to death—Brutus, his own adopted son. You sure can't trust anyone in a city like ours!

There are many statues of Caesar. His picture appears on coins, and there are monuments that bear his name. And, of course, there's the calendar. He rearranged it so that it divides the year into 365 days, and it marks all the holidays. I try not to miss any of them!

Now it's your turn. Come on, tell me about some of *your* heroes—I'm all ears!

Giants and Other Stories

Well, in the evening, after our work is done, we all sit around the fire and listen to my grandfather tell stories from long ago, when giants lived in our land. I'll tell you a scary one. But don't worry—giants don't exist anymore!

Once upon a time, there was a boy named Skjold. One day, he went hunting with the adults in the great forest. Suddenly an enormous bear came toward him looking like it wanted to kill him. Skjold had no weapons, but he was quicker than the bear. He immediately took off his belt, tied it around the bear's mouth so that the bear could not bite, threw the bear to the ground, and held it down until the adults came and killed it.

Later, Skjold became chief of many tribes. He was a generous, noble, and just leader. He won the hand of a girl named Alvilde in a fight to the death with another chief named Skate. They married and had a son, Gram, who became even more famous than his father.

Gram fell in love with Gra, the daughter of a cruel chief who had already promised her hand in marriage to a giant. Furious, Gram disguised himself as a giant and traveled to the village to confront the chief.

While walking in the forest, he met Gra. He scared her half to death! He immediately took off his disguise, and she fell in love with him. But how could they marry?

Gram and Gra asked the wizards for help. The wizards told them that Gra's nasty father could only be defeated with gold. But Gram didn't have any golden weapons, so he colored a club gold and beat the cruel chief and his soldiers. Wasn't that clever?!

A Ferocious Tortoise

Do you want to know how our Roman soldiers live? Their camps look like real villages. You don't believe me? Let's go see.

There's our camp. It's built in the shape of a rectangle with two main streets: the *cardo* and the *decumanus*. See that ditch? It was dug all around for protection. The camp is also defended by a wall with four gates, one on each side.

Look how luxurious the general's tent is! It's the one in the middle, right in front of the altar where all the soldiers sacrifice animals to the gods just before going off to fight.

The other tents are for the officials and special troops. Then there are the stables, the animal sheds, and tents for the soldiers, the slaves, and everyone else who's traveling with the army, like cooks, doctors, and craftsmen.

You can see many soldiers in their armor. They're wearing helmets and carrying swords, lances, javelins, shields, and other arms. You probably know a lot about them, since your father trades in Roman arms.

The soldiers use their shields to protect themselves from blows. They also use them to make a very strange formation called a *tortoise*. I'll draw it for you. Doesn't it look just like a funny turtle? But it's actually a kind of human fortress that helps the soldiers to conquer our enemies.

I don't like this highly organized army at all. The men have to live so far from home! And after twenty or thirty very hard years of work defending the empire, they're given only a little piece of land to live on with their families. Is that how it is in your land?

Mosquitoes at War

Well, yes, for us fighting battles is also important. We have many, many tribes and chiefs who try to conquer the lands of other peoples. And then there are you Romans—spread out across the land like an ocean wave. So we must defend ourselves, you understand?

This is how one of our soldiers dresses for combat. Naturally, he wears trousers, a tunic, a cloak, and his arms. He uses some of his arms—his bow and arrows, and his javelin—from a distance, when he's in an open field, far from the enemy. But for fighting in the forest, close to the enemy, he needs his sword, his shield, and his lance.

Some soldiers wear armor made of many iron rings to protect themselves against arrows and blows. And they wear huge helmets that weigh a ton!

Even our women help. They are the "fans." If the battle is going well, they shout for joy, and if it's going badly, they cry out in desperation. When the men hear the women's cries, they become even more combative and courageous. They know that if they lose the battle, their families will be taken prisoners and will become slaves. For us, nothing could be worse.

Now I'll share a secret with you: our soldiers attack quickly and create confusion in the enemy army. Do you know what we're like? Like a swarm of mosquitoes, ready to bite wherever we can—*bzzz!*—and then we're gone, before you know what's hit you! Don't laugh! You know very well how annoying mosquitoes can be! And they're bloodthirsty, too. You don't believe it? *Bzzz—bzzz—bzzz!*

The Ship of My Dreams

What would you like to be when you grow up? I would like to build ships. But not those little toy boats I used to play with. I'm talking about real ships, the ones that sail to faraway places!

My father says that in order to be a good shipbuilder, you have to know how to measure something by sight. You have to have a steady hand. And you have to know how to select the right wood: oak or pine.

But you can't just go into the forest and knock down a tree. You have to find the perfect tree with just the right measurements, judging by sight. Then you have to cut the tree down and bring it to the village. There it's cut with a steady hand into both long and short planks to build the hull, the deck, and all the rest of the ship.

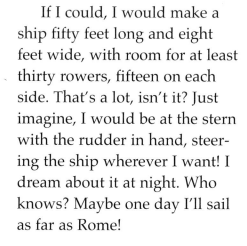

If I could, I would make a ship fifty feet long and eight feet wide, with room for at least thirty rowers, fifteen on each side. That's a lot, isn't it? Just imagine, I would be at the stern with the rudder in hand, steering the ship wherever I want! I dream about it at night. Who knows? Maybe one day I'll sail as far as Rome!

Over the Water as Far as Rome

My grandfather told me a little about ships. Near Rome there is a port called Ostia. Cargo ships arrive there from all over the empire loaded with goods and products—ivory, prized marbles, fabrics, grains and spices, even wild animals for our games and shows!

From the port of Ostia, the cargo is transferred to boats that go up the Tiber River all the way into the city. Of course, going upstream is hard. But the Romans are clever. They use mules, oxen, and buffalo to drag the boats with ropes from the banks.

Our battleships have three rows of oars and are called *triremes*. I'll tell you a story. A long time ago, the Romans were at war with the people of Carthage, who were very able sailors. The Roman soldiers weren't as powerful on sea as they were on land, so they invented the "raven"—a movable, raised bridge with iron tips as sharp as the fangs of a tiger. As soon as an enemy ship came near—*zap!*—the raven would swoop down and capture it. Then the Romans climbed aboard the ship and fought as if they were on land! And from what I've told you, can you guess who won?

Music to Send You Flying!

Do know what *I'd* like to be when I grow up? A dancer! My favorite dancers who perform during our banquets at home are Phaedra and Isidina. They seem to fly to the sounds of the harp.

What? You don't know what a harp is?! It's an instrument made of strings that you strum with your fingers. It makes a sweet, melodious sound, and it's very popular in Rome. It's fantasy music, and it gives me wings! Like the music of a flute, or panpipe.

An ancient legend says that the panpipe was invented by the god Pan, who was madly in love with the beautiful nymph, Syrinx. But Syrinx didn't want to have anything to do with the ugly Pan. She asked the gods to change her into a reed. And so they did. Poor Pan! He plucked the reed, made several little pipes of different sizes, and glued them together with tree resin. When he blew inside, out came a sweet, divine sound. And so Pan called his instrument a *syrinx*, in memory of his lost love.

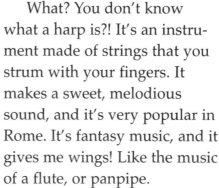

Isn't that a romantic story? But wait, where have you gone? Hmm, I hear a strange whistle. . . .

Don't Plug Your Ears!

Martilla! Martilla! Come listen! Do you know what I'm playing? No, it's not a snail! It's a flute! Look, on the top there's a hole and I blow inside of it, like this—*pfuiiit! pfuiiit!*

Every now and then I carve little flutes from willow branches. A nutshell also works, or an empty snail shell. Sometimes I use blades of grass, or a birch leaf. Musical instruments grow just about everywhere!

At home I have a tiny flute that I carved from a goat's bone. But nobody can stand to listen to it, and they cover their ears with their hands! Then I go into the forest, near the peat bog, and there I play for the gods.

I even have a special instrument for calling forth the gods: a buzzer. It's a piece of flat wood with a string attached. I whip it around fast until it makes a hissing sound, like the buzzing of a swarm of bees. It's a mysterious and exciting sound.

Would you like to have a buzzer? I'll make one just for you. Maybe you could use it to call Rufola. Come on, let's see if it works.

Have You Met Odin and Tyr?

Martilla, have you ever been near a peat bog early in the morning or in the evening at sunset? No? Well, if you ever get the chance, you'll notice that there's a strange light in the air, and everything is wrapped in a mysterious mist. I think that's where the gods are.

And since the gods live in nature, we pray to them in the open, not at an altar.

Sometimes we offer things to our gods, like a real bull, in exchange for food and riches. Other times, we use bronze images of bulls, made by the village blacksmith. They have big horns, huge bodies, and they seem very lifelike. And, boy, are they ever heavy! We offer these little bulls to Tyr, the god of war. He helps us to defeat our enemies. Tyr is always very busy.

But the wisest of all the gods is Odin. He's so powerful that he can see and hear everything. My father and I offered sacrifices to him before we started out on this trip.

We gave him a beautiful knife carved with some magic symbols, which we wrapped in a piece of cloth and then dropped into the peat bog. Odin must have liked it very much, because as you can see, he has led us this far!

You know something, Martilla? Some of those symbols look like the letters you Romans use. We call them *runes*. When we grow up, maybe we can learn what the mysterious symbols mean, and then we, too, can speak with the gods!

The Whims of the Gods

We have powerful gods, too. It seems that we have more gods in Rome than days of the year! I could go on for a month telling you about them!

Everywhere there are temples dedicated to the gods, where the priests perform the sacred rites.

Our gods are pictured with human forms. They have a lot of powers, but they're not perfect. Just imagine, some of them get into arguments, get jealous, get angry, and do things out of spite, just like we humans do!

The father and king of all the gods is Jupiter, and he has a wife named Juno. When Jupiter is angry he throws lightning bolts from the sky. Then you pray that you'll be spared! Everyone tries to appease him with ceremonies and sacrifices.

Then there's Minerva, the wise goddess who protects our city. And Mars, the god of war. My name comes from his, although I'm always cheerful and peaceful, and I like making friends with everyone. Do you know why Mars is very famous in Rome? He's the father of Romulus, the founder of our city.

The most beautiful is Venus, the goddess of love. She's adored and courted, and poets and lovers always call to her. Her son is just as famous as she is: little Cupid with his magic arrows. He shoots just one, and whoever he hits falls madly in love!

To have the protection of the gods, and to make them happy, we sacrifice animals to them — sheep, rams, pigs, and bulls — just like you do!

A Frightening Dream

Today I'm very sad. There's something strange in the air. It must be these black clouds and the low-flying birds. But I have a terrible feeling—an omen that something bad is about to happen.

We believe in omens and dreams. And last night I had a frightening dream. When I woke up, I was drenched in sweat in the pitch dark of the tent. Next to me an old woman had her mouth open, and she seemed dead—even though I could hear her breathing.

Dead people spook me! We bury them outside the city walls. The richest ones have family tombs that are like beautiful monuments, full of writings and decorations. Poor people are buried in a wooden box.

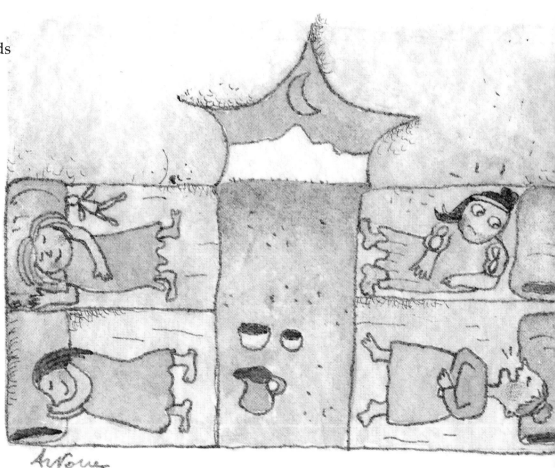

But first there's the funeral. The dead person is carried around on a stretcher. He's followed by his relatives, tuba players, and women who cry and mourn. Sometimes a guy wearing a strange mask follows behind them. He pretends to be one of the dead person's ancestors who'll accompany him on his journey to the Underworld, which is the kingdom of the dead.

If someone doesn't get a proper burial, there's really reason to be afraid! His spirit won't find any peace. It'll wander around lost and angry with the living. Then nothing you do to keep it away will work. It may appear as an evil spirit, or with a great clanking noise, and then suddenly disappear. *Brrr!!!* I tremble just thinking about it!

But you have a strange and sad expression, Marbord. Don't tell me you had a bad dream, too!

Saying Goodbye Is a Little Like Dying

No, but last night my father gave me some bad news: your troops are preparing to enter Germany. Do you know what that means? Soon there'll be another war between our people, and many will die, even women and children.

Where I come from, there are different ways of burying our dead. Some people burn the body of the dead person together with gifts that he or she will use in the afterworld. The ashes and bones are then collected in an urn, which is buried beneath a small mound of earth or stones. A few objects are placed next to the burial spot—a bowl of food, something to drink, and a knife that can be offered to the gods. With all of the wars going on, our god Odin must have thousands of knives!

Other people are buried in wooden boxes filled with all of their favorite things, especially precious objects such as necklaces, rings, and bracelets. I would definitely have with me my beloved flute, but I hope this is still many, many years away! I want to live, Martilla!

I still have so many things to do and see! I want to have my own horse and I want to build ships that will sail as far as Rome. I also want to find out how those heating systems of yours work—then I'll be the first in our village not to be cold in the winter!

Now we must leave, or your people will think we are enemy spies! The cart's ready and my father's calling me. We must hurry, or your soldiers will capture us and take us back with them to Rome as slaves. I wouldn't like that!

A City Half of Slaves

I'm sorry you have to go, Marbord. I'll miss you. You're lucky that you're not a slave. I suppose I'm lucky, too, because some slaves in Rome are much worse off than I am. My master treats me and my family very well—we have clothes to wear, food to eat, and a nice place to live. Except, of course, when we have to travel with the army!

In Rome, almost half of the city are slaves. Can you imagine? Slaves are needed to build roads, houses, and bridges; to farm and do housework; and to travel with the army—like my family. Some slaves are gladiators, fighting for their lives against beasts and men in the amphitheater. Greek slaves often raise the master's children because the Greeks are considered very smart.

Some slaves come from far-away lands as prisoners of war. Sometimes poor people become slaves to a wealthier person. Even little babies can become slaves, if their fathers don't accept them into the family. Many of these babies are girls, who are not considered as useful as boys. I don't believe in that—where would Rufola be without me? And where would my master be without Rufola's milk?

If I'm very lucky, maybe one day my master will give me the gift of freedom. Then I can do what all the other free people in Rome do. Or maybe I'll save all of my money and buy my freedom when I'm older. But I'm afraid that as long as there are wars, slaves like me will always be needed.

What do you think is worse — being a slave or a barbarian?

Slavery Is . . . Barbarian

Being a slave *is* barbarian, Martilla! And I don't agree with how the Romans treat their slaves. Or how they make prisoners into slaves. Or how they buy and sell people, or make newborn babies slaves. To me that sounds . . . well, barbarian.

Although we, too, have slaves, they're not really like the slaves in Rome. We call our slaves serfs. They're treated differently than Roman slaves. In my land, it's very, very unusual for a master to beat his serf. A serf costs a lot of money, so it's silly to hurt him, isn't it? It's much better to treat him well, so that he can live long and work in the fields, take care of the animals, and make his master rich.

My father once told me a story about a man in our town. He was young and very strong, but not very clever. One day at the town fair he played dice with other free men. Do you know what he did? He gambled away all his belongings. First he lost his animals, then his house, and then everything else he owned. In the end, he only had himself left, and now he doesn't even have that, because now he's a serf. Do you know who his master is? The man who won him playing dice!

I must go now, Martilla. Don't forget me! Tell your friends that we "barbarians" are not so strange after all! Say goodbye to Rufola for me. I'll see you in Rome!

Who's a Barbarian?

Goodbye, Marbord! Maybe some day you'll come to Rome and visit me. You'll be a famous shipbuilder and I'll be a dancer. Maybe I'll even be free!

I'll remember what I've learned about you and your people. It's funny—to me you're not a "barbarian" any-more. It's true that you look and act a little strange, but that just means that we're different.

Look—no one's around. I'll race you to your cart. Last one there's a . . . barbarian!

Scandia

Oceanus
Atlanticus

Fionia

Colonia

Mogontiaeum

Mediolanum

Roma

Mare Internum

Artoue L.

Glossary

amphitheater An open space surrounded by many levels of seats where public games and contests were held.

atrium The courtyard in the middle of a Roman house. It is surrounded on all four sides by the house, and it is open to the sky.

barbarian The Roman name for those who did not speak Latin. To Romans, the language of barbarians sounded like "bah-bah-bar," and the word "barbarian" comes from that sound.

Brutus A Roman politician and nobleman who helped kill Julius Caesar.

bulla An amulet, or charm, often made of gold, that was worn by Roman children from good families until they grew up.

calceus A Roman leather shoe that covered the whole foot and ankle, unlike sandals, which covered only the soles of the feet.

capsa A box or case for keeping books or scrolls.

cardo A main street that ran through a Roman military camp or town.

Carthage An ancient city on the north coast of Africa. The Carthaginians were enemies of the Romans. The Romans fought several wars with them.

Cleopatra The Queen of Egypt who was a friend and at times an enemy of the Romans. She was the lover of several important Romans and had a son with Julius Caesar.

Cupid The Roman god of love.

De Bello Gallico The book by Julius Caesar— *Gallic Wars*— that describes how he fought against the Gauls (in what is now France), finally conquered them, and made them part of the Roman Empire.

decumanus A main street that ran through a Roman military camp or town. It ran perpendicularly to the cardo.

domus The city house of a wealthy Roman.

ferula A wooden stick that was used by schoolteachers to discipline their students.

fibula A pin or clasp that holds clothes in place. It may be very simple and made of bronze, or it may be very elaborate and made of silver or gold and decorated with amber or precious stones.

focaccia bread Italian bread baked flat and sometimes flavored with herbs and olive oil.

forum The open square or market place in a town. Important public buildings were often located around the forum.

fresco A wall painting with water-based colors that was made while the plaster on the wall was still damp.

Gaul The Roman name for the land that is now France and for a person who lived there.

gladiators Men who staged fights, sometimes until death, in the arenas, as public entertainment for the Romans.

Julius Caesar The Roman general and politician who was a ruler of Rome. When he became too powerful, the nobles conspired to kill him in 44 B.C.

Juno The powerful Roman goddess who was associated with women, warfare, and fertility.

Jupiter The supreme Roman god who was associated with the sky, storms, lightning, and power.

Latin The language spoken by the Romans.

latrina A bath or bathhouse.

Marcus Aurelius A Roman emperor and philosopher.

Mars The Roman god of war.

mead An alcoholic drink that was made from water, honey, malt, and yeast.

Minerva The Roman goddess of knowledge and wisdom.

mosaic — Decorative pictures or patterns for floors or walls that were made of small pieces of colored stone or glass set in cement.

Odin — The main god of the Germanic peoples.

omen — A warning sign or a prediction of things to come.

Ostia — The town where Rome's harbor was located.

Pan — The Greek god of shepherds and flocks of sheep and goats. He was half-goat and half-man.

panpipe — A pipe made from reeds of different lengths that were tied together. Supposedly it was the invention of the god Pan.

peat bog — Swampy and damp earth that was once a lake.

peristyle — A garden surrounded by a row of columns supporting a roof over a path that goes all the way around the garden.

public baths — Large buildings with elaborate public baths that were built by the emperor in Roman towns. Men and women went there every day both to bathe and to meet friends.

Roman Empire — The part of the ancient world that was under the rule of Rome. Its size varied, for there were always wars at its borders. Its largest area stretched from England in the north to North Africa and Egypt in the south, and from Spain in the west to Turkey, Israel, and Jordan in the east.

Rome — The city at the center of the Roman Empire from which the empire was ruled. Today it is the capital of Italy.

Romulus — The legendary founder of the city of Rome.

runes — The alphabet system that was used to write Old Norse, the ancient language of Scandia. Because most people were unable to read, the letters were thought to have magical powers.

Scandia — The area that is now Denmark and southern Sweden.

serf — Someone who has to live on land that is owned by his master and work for the master when he demands it.

stola — A long, pleated dress that was worn by wealthy Roman women.

stylus — A pointed stick that was used by Roman students for writing.

Syrinx — The beautiful nymph, or maiden, who was changed into a reed in order to escape the god Pan.

Tiber River — The river that runs through the city of Rome to her port city of Ostia.

toga — A large piece of fabric in the shape of a half-moon that Roman men wore over their other clothes in public for ceremonial occasions. It was wrapped around their bodies and folded over their left arms.

tortoise — In this formation, a group of Roman foot soldiers stood very close to each other and held their shields close together to cover themselves completely on the sides and on the top. This allowed them to attack their enemy—somewhat like a modern tank.

trireme — A Roman battleship that was rowed by men who sat in three rows, one above another.

tunic — A simple kneelength garment with or without sleeves, like a sweater, worn by both Roman men and women. It could be worn with or without a belt.

Tyr — The Germanic god of war.

Underworld — The place where Romans believed dead souls went.

Venus — The Roman goddess of love.

About the Authors and Illustrators

Birgitta Petrén
is the author of several popular books on
the history of the Scandinavian people.
She lives in Sweden.

Elisabetta Putini
is the author of several children's books.
She lives in Rome.

Lara Artone and Monica Barsotti
are children's book illustrators.
They studied graphics at the European
Institute for Design. They live in Rome.